Unicorn Races

Written by Stephen J. Brooks
Illustrated by Linda Crockett

~ For Rylee Annabelle Brooks ~
May you always believe in the power of dreams and remember to follow your heart.

copyright © 2007 Stephen J. Brooks
illustrations © 2007 Linda Crockett

Book design & layout by Phat Vuong
phatvuong.com

PURPLE SKY PUBLISHING
PO Box 12013, Parkville, MO 64152 • www.purpleskypublishing.com

Printed in China
SAN 256-5994

LCCN: 2005906800

Publisher's Cataloging-In-Publication Data
(Prepared by The Donohue Group, Inc.)

Brooks, Stephen (Stephen J.)
    Unicorn races / written by Stephen J. Brooks ; illustrated by Linda Crockett.

    p. : col. ill. ; cm.

    Summary: Princess Abigail travels to a magical glade where a great unicorn race is held.
    ISBN-13: 978-0-9769017-3-0
    ISBN-10: 0-9769017-3-0

1. Unicorns--Juvenile fiction. 2. Racing--Juvenile fiction. 3. Imagination--Juvenile fiction. 4. Unicorns--Fiction. 5. Racing--Fiction. 6. Imagination--Fiction. I. Crockett-Blassingame, Linda, 1948- II. Title.

PZ7.B7599 Un 2007
[E]   2005906800

As she did each and every night, when her mother had tucked her in bed, kissed her good night and wished her pleasant dreams; Abigail closed her eyes, pretending to be asleep.

She waited until she heard her mother's fading footsteps before she opened one eye, then the other. The only sound in the room was the ticking of the clock: "Tick Tock, Tick Tock, Tick Tock." Abigail rose from her bed ready for adventure.

As quietly as a mouse, Abigail put on her favorite princess dress. She donned her princess shoes and waved her princess wand.

"What a night this shall be!" she said out loud as she opened the window and peered out into the darkness. "Lord William," she whispered, "Lord William, your princess awaits."

"Tardy as usual," she thought to herself as she returned to her preparations.

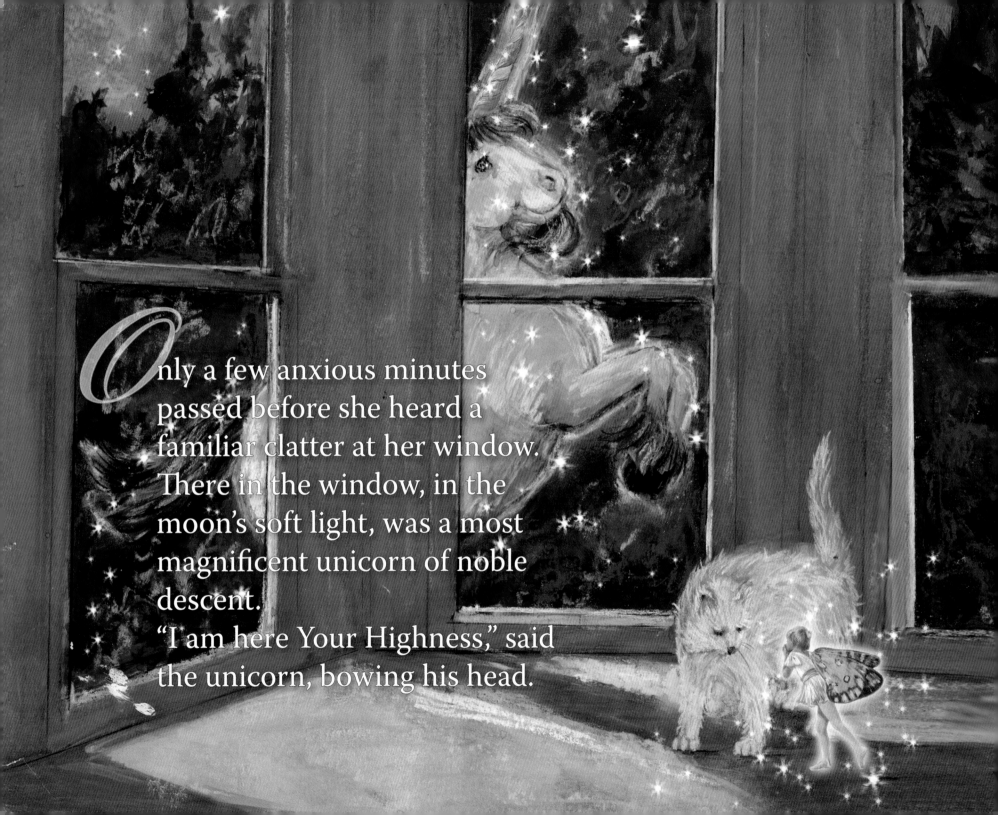

Only a few anxious minutes passed before she heard a familiar clatter at her window. There in the window, in the moon's soft light, was a most magnificent unicorn of noble descent.

"I am here Your Highness," said the unicorn, bowing his head.

"And I am ready!" said young Abigail as she put on her princess crown.

"You are late," Abigail softly scolded as she climbed on his back. "Then let us go...the races will soon start," answered Lord William as the regal pair took flight.

"To the races!" Abigail declared.

As they flew off into the night, the world turned small and Abigail's house was soon out of sight. They traveled swiftly through the darkness with the cool night breeze speeding their way. Soon, the noble unicorn turned and said, "We are almost there Your Highness!"

"Hooray!" shouted the young princess.

Lord William and the majestic princess soon arrived at a brightly lit clearing. "We are here!" announced the unicorn as he swept low and gently landed. Abigail dismounted and adjusted her royal crown. "Your Highness," said the unicorn, "your throne awaits."

There in the deep of the woods, by a slow moving stream, was a royal feast prepared by elves and fairies of cookies and cakes and ice cream sundaes with cherries.

"No treats until the race is won," Abigail commanded as she prepared to take her place at her royal throne.

The young princess looked around at her eager contestants. She counted six unicorns in all this night: purple, pink, blue, green, yellow and white. "Quite a race we shall have," she thought to herself.

The unicorns rose up, neighing and huffing, ready for the race to begin. "Take your mark and we shall get started," declared Abigail.

The magnificent creatures stood side by side waiting for their command. "Such a beautiful sight," the princess said with a smile.

Abigail took a deep breath and then shouted as loud as she could: "On your mark, get ready, get set and go!" The elves and fairies let out a cheer.

In a flash, the six majestic unicorns quickly bolted from the clearing. Like a rainbow after a mid-summer's shower, the colorful beasts stretched across the shadowy skyline. The princess watched in astonishment as they gracefully took flight.

The unicorns raced neck and neck to the second bright star. They turned and circled the moon twice, and flew on through the night. "Go, go, go!" Abigail yelled out. They raced low to the ground. They raced high in the sky. "They are almost done!" Abigail cried.

They raced to the ocean's edge and ran among the white-capped waves. They followed the sandy shoreline past the menacing rocky cliffs. They ran to the lighthouse that stood tall in the night. Then, they turned and headed back to the clearing, with the fairies, the elves and Abigail cheering.

The galloping group crossed the finish line with the race seemingly too close to call. The audience of onlookers stood in anxious silence as the princess sat in thought, then raised up and happily declared, "Blue won!"

A roar went up from the festive crowd as the princess adorned the unicorn with the traditional wreath of yellow roses.
"Let the party begin," Abigail decreed.

There in that clearing, on this magical night, a feast of cookies and cakes and sundaes took place, all in honor of the great unicorn race. "Hooray for Princess Abigail!" all cried.

While her subjects celebrated under the moon's soft glow, Abigail and Lord William flew off into the night. They flew until they could no longer see the magical clearing and the voices and cheering of the fairies and elves were but whispers on the wind.

They flew back to young Abigail's room where she tiptoed back to bed, quiet as a mouse. "Good night Lord William," Abigail softly whispered. Abigail rested her head and drifted off to sleep, exhausted from her night. Still wearing her crown and with a smile on her face, Abigail dreamt of the next great unicorn race.

"Good night my princess…good night."